One Way

Norah McClintock

orca soundings

ORCA BOOK PUBLISHERS

Library and Archives Canada Cataloguing in Publication

McClintock, Norah
One way / Norah McClintock.
(Orca soundings)

Issued also in electronic formats.
ISBN 978-1-4598-0173-8 (bound).--ISBN 978-1-4598-0172-1 (pbk.)

I. Title. II. Series: Orca soundings.
PS8575.C62064 2012 JC813'.54 C2011-907851-1

First published in the United States, 2012
Library of Congress Control Number: 2011943729

Summary: When Kenzie critically injures his ex-girlfriend, suspicion grows that it was not an accident, and his behavior seems to confirm it.

Orca Book Publishers is dedicated to preserving the environment and has printed this book on paper certified by the Forest Stewardship Council®.

Orca Book Publishers gratefully acknowledges the support for its publishing programs provided by the following agencies: the Government of Canada through the Canada Book Fund and the Canada Council for the Arts, and the Province of British Columbia through the BC Arts Council and the Book Publishing Tax Credit.

Cover photography by Getty Images

ORCA BOOK PUBLISHERS
PO Box 5626, Stn. B
Victoria, BC Canada
V8R 6S4

ORCA BOOK PUBLISHERS
PO Box 468
Custer, WA USA
98240-0468

www.orcabook.com
Printed and bound in Canada.

15 14 13 12 • 4 3 2 1

Chapter One

I'm not going fast when I round the corner on my bike. In fact, it seems like I'm crawling along. But what happens next reminds me of the time my dad and I drove home in a rainstorm.

The wind was vicious that night. It uprooted trees. The rain didn't just fall, it hammered down at a forty-five-degree angle. My dad should have pulled over and waited for the storm to calm down. But we were ten minutes away from the house, and he was worried about the roof, which was in bad shape to begin with. Even if it had blown right off our house, there was nothing he could have done about it. Still, he was determined to get home as fast as possible.

We came to the sharp turn in the road just around the corner from our house. I can still see my dad gripping the steering wheel like it was a life preserver and he was adrift on in the middle of the ocean. But it didn't do any good, not with all that wind and rain and the deep puddles where the road surface was uneven. The next thing we knew, the car was skimming over the top of a huge puddle. The tires had no traction. My dad had no control. The car slid off the road, hit the ditch and rolled over. Altogether, the whole thing took ten seconds. But it felt like ten minutes.

Even now, if I close my eyes, I can see it as if it's a movie. I see the car going sideways instead of forward. I see my dad's head turn, first to look where we're going and then to look at me. There's a look of terror on his face, and it scares me. Then I feel his side of the car drop and my side rise. As I watch, everything turns upside down and then right-side up again. The car slams onto the Ormistons' front yard. I sit there, staring out into the dark night and the hammering rain, which is no match for my hammering heart. I test my legs, my arms, my neck. I'm in one piece. Nothing even hurts. I look at my dad. He's okay too, but he's as shaken up as I am.

Well, what happens to me after I round the corner on my bike is a lot like what happened in the car that night. It isn't raining, and there's no wind. But a few seconds after I make my turn, everything kicks into slow motion.

I make the corner, heading up on Brannigan so that I can park my bike and lock it up in front of the school. There's no traffic, but there is a white delivery van parked halfway up the street, just this side of the school. I'm going to have to pass it on my way to lock up my bike.

It's halfway through lunch period, but it's a cool day for early May, so there aren't as many kids on the street as there would be if it was, say, a nice warm day. I see a knot of guys up the street on the other side of the school, their backs to me. I see Stoner across the street from school, holding his phone as far from his face as he can, doing one of his rants. I see a whole bunch of girls standing around talking about whatever girls talk about. I see Logan McCann coming down the school steps. He sees me and smirks. He always smirks when he sees me.

A car passes me, headed south. The driver looks startled when he sees me coming his way. He points back over his shoulder like he's trying to jab someone in the backseat, but there's no one there. I just shrug. He gives me the finger, so I figure he's one of those anti-bike maniacs who probably foams at the mouth whenever he's stuck in traffic and a cyclist breezes past him. I glance over my shoulder to return the favor, but he's already turned the corner. I'm just straightening up again when it happens.

I hit something.

I have no idea what it is. All I know is that my bike slams to such a sudden stop that my butt comes off the seat and my feet leave the pedals. But I continue to grip the handlebars because I have the crazy idea that if I just hang on, everything will be okay.

I realize I'm wrong about that at the same time I realize I'm upside down. In fact, before I know it, my feet are so high up in the air that it looks like I'm standing on a cloud.

Then I feel myself flipping over.

I let go of the handlebars, not that it makes any difference. My legs have arced over my head and are starting to come down again. A moment later, I'm stretched out straight, like I'm lying on an invisible bed. I see that that's how I'm going to hit the pavement—flat on my back. I think, Thank god I'm wearing a helmet, which, believe me, is something I never think. Mostly I think that helmets are for wusses.

My legs continue to fall, and the top part of my body starts to right itself. For a moment I think I'm going to land on my feet—*ta-DA*! But I don't. I splat onto the ground.

Except it isn't the ground that I land on. It's something kind of lumpy. My bike falls on top of me.

Maybe I'm out for a few seconds. Maybe I'm out longer. I don't know.

But I'm definitely out cold, because when I open my eyes, there are people crowded around me, and I can't figure out where they came from. I hear someone say, "Do you think she's alive?" I think, What an idiot! In the first place, you could be Einstein's half-witted brother and still tell at a glance that I'm a guy, not a girl. In the second place, when was the last time you saw a dead person open his eyes?

I blink a couple of times. My head is pounding. I hurt everywhere—my back, my legs, my arms.

Someone starts to lift the bike off me.

Someone else says, "Maybe you should leave it where it is, you know, for the cops."

A third person says, "They're sending an ambulance."

Another person, a girl, is crying.

The first two people are arguing about whether or not to leave my bike on top of me when all of a sudden it's lifted off me. I look up and see my best friend T.J.

"Hey, Kenz, are you okay?" he says. Then he looks at whatever I landed on, and his face goes pale.

I'm trying to sit up when the ambulance arrives and the paramedics push their way through the crowd. They stop and stare for a moment. Two cops in uniform show up. The four of them—the two paramedics and the two cops—talk for a few seconds. Then the cops start taking charge of the crowd, telling everyone to move back. One of the paramedics asks me if I can move. I say yes. He tells me to lie still all the same because they're going to lift me off the girl.

Girl? What girl?

Before I can ask, I'm being strapped onto a board, hoisted into the air and put down again, gently. That's when I see her—the girl.

It's Stassi.

Her eyes are closed. She's not moving. There's blood under her head, and she is lying partly on the edge of the sidewalk and partly on the road. One of the paramedics presses a stethoscope to her chest. Before I can find out what he hears—or doesn't hear—the second paramedic kneels down beside me, blocking my view and asking me questions while he checks me out.

It turns out I haven't broken anything, at least, not as far as they can tell. They want to take me to the hospital for a thorough examination. They want to know my name and who they should call.

More cops arrive and talk to the two who are already there. I hear the word *victim*.

Chapter Two

As soon as I hear that word—*victim*—I try to get up. That's how addled I am. I completely forget that I am strapped to a board.

The paramedic must think I'm freaking out, because he tries to calm me down. I tell him I want to get up. I tell him I *have* to get up, I have to see what happened. He tells me to "Take it easy, partner." He keeps telling me that until I am loaded into the ambulance

The next thing I know, I'm at the hospital. Everything is a blur. A doctor is telling me I'm lucky that nothing is broken but that I'm going to feel some pain because I'm going to have a lot of bruises. My mom is there. A doctor is telling her to keep an eye on me because it's possible I have a concussion. A nurse gives her a sheet of paper that lists what my mom should look out for and what she should do if anything on the sheet happens.

Then there are cops in the room, only this time they introduce themselves as detectives. They want to ask me about "the incident." They're super friendly. They ask how I'm feeling. They tell me it's a good thing I was wearing a helmet and that I'd be surprised how many times they see people who aren't and what happens to them when their heads hit the concrete.

That's when I start to shake all over, because all of a sudden I'm remembering Stassi's head, which also hit the pavement. I saw it. I saw her eyes closed. I saw the pool of blood under her. I hope she's okay. I hope it looks worse than it really is.

The cops ask me to tell them what I remember. I'm just getting started when my dad rushes into the cubicle.

"I heard what happened," he says to my mom. He's gasping for breath. He must have run in from the parking lot. "Is he—?" His eyes find me. He looks me over and relaxes. "Kenzie, are you okay?"

"The doctor says he's fine," my mom assures him. "These detectives need to ask him some questions."

"Detectives?" My dad frowns. "I was told it was an accident."

"We need to get everything straight," one of the cops says. I notice he doesn't agree with my dad. But he doesn't say he's wrong either.

My mom puts a hand on my dad's arm. My dad nods at the cops.

"Okay," he says.

"Do you remember which direction you were riding, Kenzie?" one of the detectives asks.

"Up toward the school."

"That's north, right?" he says. "North on Brannigan?"

"I guess," I say.

"Are you sure about that? This is important, Kenzie," the other detective says.

My dad is listening carefully.

"I guess it was north," I say. I've never been great with directions. Mostly I navigate by left and right.

"You were riding toward school, and you turned onto Brannigan from Fifth Street, right?" the same detective asks.

"Yeah."

The two detectives look at each other. My dad shakes his head.

"You can't be serious," he says. "You're giving my son grief because he rode his bicycle the wrong way up a one-way street?"

"It's against the law," the detective says.

"It's a *bicycle*," my dad says.

"He hit a girl."

Not just *a* girl. I hit Stassi.

"A girl who stepped out into the street in front of him without looking both ways to see if anything was coming," my dad says. "Isn't that right, son?"

"Dave, it was Stassi," my mom says quietly.

My dad absorbs this.

"Stassi Mikalchuk?" my dad says, as if he knows hundreds of Stassis and wants to make sure which one she's talking about.

"Stassi *Mikalczyk*," my mom says. My dad never gets her name right.

"Is she all right?" my dad asks.

My mom says she doesn't know. The cops don't know either. Or, if they do, they don't say.

"Still, when you step out onto the street, you should look both ways," my dad says. "You avoid a lot of accidents that way."

My mother squeezes my hand, hard, and that's when it hits me. The best way to prevent the kind of accident I just had is to not ride the wrong way up a one-way street because, really, why would anyone look *both* ways when traffic is only supposed to be going *one* way?

"Why don't we step outside for a moment, sir?" one of the detectives says to my dad. "So we can talk."

My dad doesn't want to. I can tell by how stiff his body is and by the sour look on his face. But he steps outside with them anyway. They must move down the hall because I can't hear what they're saying, which is fine with me. My head is pounding. It's like someone has turned a couple of monkeys loose with jackhammers and they've decided that it's more fun to punch holes in a human skull than it is to tear up a road. I close my eyes. The pounding gets worse.

When my dad comes back, he's alone. He comes and stands beside my mom. He rests his hand on her shoulder and says to me, "You're not to talk to the police, you understand me, Kenzie?"

"Why?" my mom says. "What's the matter, Dave?"

She's as scared as I am by the look on his face.

"Is Stassi all right?" I ask.

"Dave, what's wrong?" my mom says.

"Is she okay?" I ask again. "Is Stassi okay?"

My dad's face is grim. "She's in surgery," he says.

Chapter Three

The hospital releases me. I walk out of Emergency with my parents. The two detectives have left. We go straight to the car and drive home. My mom takes me upstairs to my room and makes me change into my pajamas and get into bed. I hear the soft rumble of my dad's voice downstairs. He's talking on the phone. My mom goes downstairs.

She wants to make me some chicken noodle soup, just like she used to do when I was little and had to stay home sick from school. I try to tell her I'm not hungry, but she says that's nonsense, the soup will do me good. I lie in my bed thinking about Stassi and listening to my parents whisper down below.

Footsteps.

It's not my mom with the soup. It's my dad. "Howard is going to come over later," he says. He means Howard Grossman. Mr. Grossman and my dad play golf together. Mr. Grossman is a lawyer.

"Why?" I ask. "It was an accident, Dad. I didn't mean to hit her. I would never hurt Stassi."

"I know," my dad says. "It's just a precaution. In case the police decide to charge you with something."

"Charge me?" I feel panicky inside. "With what?"

"Howard thinks possibly careless driving."

"But I was on my bike, Dad."

"A bike is a vehicle. Howard says bikes are covered under the Highway Traffic Act. But he's pretty sure careless driving is the worst they can charge you with."

The *worst*?

Pretty sure?

"The important thing is, he doesn't want you talking to anyone about what happened."

"But it was an acc—"

"He was very clear about that, Kenzie. Don't talk to anyone, okay? You talk to Howard tonight, and then we'll let him handle it. And if the cops approach you, you tell them you're not going to talk to them without your lawyer present. And then you call Howard. Whatever you do, don't say anything to them, do you understand?"

"You're scaring me, Dad."

He smiles, just a little.

"It's a precaution, son, that's all. If there's any chance you're going to get charged with anything, it's smart to get some sound advice and then to make sure you follow that advice."

"What about Stassi? Have you heard anything?"

My dad shakes his head.

"Can you call her parents? Can you find out how she is?"

I hear the faint rattle of dishes. Dad turns.

"Here's your mother with some soup. Eat up. Get some rest. I'll let you know when Howard gets here."

"Call her parents," I tell him. "Please, Dad? I have to know if she's okay."

My dad seems reluctant, which I can't figure out. But he finally agrees. My mom sits down on the side of the bed and watches me eat a few spoonfuls of soup. My dad comes back a few moments later. My mother takes one look at him and squeezes my hand.

"Her father didn't want to talk to me," my dad says. "Her mother came on the phone though. She says Stassi is out of surgery but her condition is critical." I feel sick inside. "She asked me how you were."

Mrs. Mikalczyk was always nice to me. Her father never liked me. I think he wanted Stassi to go out with someone from the old country, someone who spoke the same language. Mrs. Mikalczyk speaks English really well, but her husband has a thick accent. I hardly ever understand him.

I think about what my dad has just told me.

"So," I say after a little while. "Is she going to be okay?"

"They don't know, son," my dad answers.

Howard Grossman shows up at eight o'clock that night. He shakes my dad's hand, kisses my mom on the cheek and swings his briefcase up onto the dining-room table. Mom and Dad sit on either side of me. Mr. Grossman takes the chair across from me.

"I've talked to the police," he says.

"And?" my dad asks.

"And they say they're still investigating."

"Investigating what?" I ask.

Mr. Grossman pulls a leather folder from his briefcase and opens it in front of him. He reaches into the breast pocket of his suit jacket and pulls out a fountain pen. It's gold-plated. Dad says Mr. Grossman does very well in his law practice. He makes out like a bandit, is how my dad puts it.

"Now then, Kenzie, suppose you walk me through exactly what happened," he says, smiling at me.

"What are they investigating?" I ask. "I don't understand."

"That will become clear in due course," Mr. Grossman says. "It could be as simple as making sure they've interviewed all the witnesses and have the facts straight in their minds."

Could be?

"In the meantime, I want to get *my* facts clear. Tell me step-by-step what happened, Kenzie."

I start to talk. He listens and jots down notes from time to time. When I've finished, he asks me a few questions, such as: "Did you realize you were going the wrong way on a one-way street?"

"I don't know," I say. "Maybe. I didn't really think about it."

"Were you aware that Brannigan is a one-way street?"

I don't know what to say. Like I said, I never really thought about it.

"I ride up it all the time," I say. "Everybody does."

"Everybody?" Mr. Grossman leans across the table toward me. "Like who?"

"I don't know. Kids at school."

"It would be helpful to have some names, Kenzie," Mr. Grossman says. "I went over there this afternoon. I noticed that the arrow indicating one way at the corner of Brannigan and Fifth is partially obstructed by the branch of a tree. If other kids—or adults, for that matter—go the wrong way up Brannigan and are unaware that it's a one-way street—"

"It's clearly marked," my mother says. "There are one-way arrows in several places up and down the street. I know. When Kenzie sprained his ankle two years ago, I had to drive him to school every morning."

Mr. Grossman stares silently at her. He glances at my dad.

"Let Howard do his job," my dad says irritably. "He's here to talk to Kenzie, not us."

"But I just thought—"

My dad cuts her off. He says, "Don't." He nods at Mr. Grossman. "Go on."

"Just walk me through what happened, Kenzie."

So I do. I tell him about getting to school late because of a dentist appointment.

"But that appointment was for nine o'clock," my mom says. "Why were you only arriving at school at noon?"

My dad shoots her another irritated look.

"Dr. Thoms was running late," I say. "And then since all I had before lunch was drama..."

"You promised me you wouldn't cut classes anymore," my mom says.

"It was *drama*," my dad says. "For crying out loud, Susie, let the kid talk."

My mother's cheeks turn pink. She stands up all of a sudden.

"Coffee, Howard?" she asks.

"That would be lovely, Susie," Mr. Grossman says. He waits until she leaves the room before turning back to me. "Now, Kenzie, I'd like you to give some thought to who else you might have seen riding the wrong way up that street. They won't get into trouble, I promise you. But it's better to be safe than sorry."

I say I'll think about it and let him know.

"Have you ever had any trouble with the police about your bike?" he asks.

I glance at my dad. "They stopped me once about a month ago," I say.

"Oh? What for?"

"I kind of blew through an intersection."

I feel my dad tense up beside me.

"An intersection marked with a stop sign?" Mr. Grossman asks.

"A red light," I mumble. "But it wasn't a real intersection. It was a T intersection. There was no way I could have got hit by a car."

Mr. Grossman peers at me from across the table.

"What did the police do?" he asks.

"They gave me a warning."

"Did they take your name?"

I nod. "They said the next time they'd ticket me. They said I could have knocked that old man over."

"What old man?" my father demands.

There's no point in hiding it, not when the cops wrote it down.

"I didn't see him," I said. "He was stepping off the curb to cross the street—"

"You had a red light," my father says, using the same irritated tone on me that he had used on my mother.

"Yeah, but—"

"For god's sake, Kenzie! Maybe they *should* charge you!"

"Do you remember where this happened?" Mr. Grossman asks.

"What difference does that make?" my dad says.

"If I know where it happened, I'll know what division it was. I can try to track down the cop who warned him. It was one cop, right, Kenzie?"

"A cop on a bike," I say. I hadn't seen him either. I tell Mr. Grossman where it happened. My dad slumps in his chair.

"If they charge him, they'll go for the max, won't they, Howard?" he says.

"The max?" I try to hide how nervous those words make me.

"It's two grand," Howard says with a shrug. "What's two grand these days?"

Two *thousand* dollars? I glance at my dad. He's glowering at me. I see my allowance fluttering away on little wings, just like in a cartoon.

"It could be worse," Mr. Grossman says. "He could have been behind the wheel of a car." He turns to me again. "About the girl who was injured—Nastasia Mikalczyk. I understand you knew her well."

Knew?

"I *know* her," I say. *Know* is present tense. She's still here. She's still alive. "She's—was—my girlfriend."

Mr Grossman arches an eyebrow and looks at my dad.

"They broke up," my dad says. "Kenzie broke up with her."

"Is that right, Kenzie? You broke up with her, not the other way around?"

"What difference does it make?" my dad wants to know.

"Just asking," Mr. Grossman says calmly. He waits for my answer.

"Yeah," I say. "That's right."

It's what I told my parents. It's what I told everyone. But it's only partly true, and the part that's true is pretty small compared to the part that's not true.

"Okay," Mr. Grossman says. He gives me his card and tells me to call him if anything happens.

"Can't I just pay the fine and get it over with?" I ask. "I mean, I *was* going the wrong way. I guess it was my fault."

"Oh," my dad says sarcastically. "You have two grand stashed somewhere that I don't know about?"

Chapter Four

You wouldn't know it from the way my dad treats her a lot of the time, but my mom's really smart. So what if she didn't finish university and my dad did? Whose fault is that? I mean, she got pregnant—with me. And you know what they say—it takes two to do *that* tango. And so what if, because of that and because she wanted to spend time with me, she doesn't have a great job like my dad does? He's an engineer. Well, sort of. He works for a chain of fast-food restaurants. His job is to do the specs for the new places they build. My mom works as a part-time receptionist at a pet-care salon. She likes the hours and loves the animals, and the animals and their owners like her. Dad, of course, has no patience for either pets or pet owners, which is why I've never been allowed to have a dog.

A lot of people, my dad included (although he'd deny it), look down on receptionists. My mom knows it. She shrugs it off. She says there are different kinds of smart. She says my dad is smart with math and science, but he's not as smart with people. My mom's a people-person. She's proud of it. And I'm proud of her. Unlike my dad, who tells people that she has a "little" job so that she can waste her money on stuff like accent pillows and scented candles, which isn't at all how she spends what she earns. But that's beside the point.

The main thing is, my mom knows people. She can read them as if they were books. And the person she can read best? You guessed it. Me.

The next morning goes like this.

Mom: You're going to be late for school, Kenz.

Me: School? I ache all over! I'm not going to school.

Mom (looking shocked even though she isn't, really): Not go to school? Correct me if I'm wrong, young man, but finals are coming up soon.

Me (groaning): They're a whole month away.

Mom: They're *only* a month away.

Me: Aw, come on, Mom. Let me take just one day off.

Mom: No way, young man.

Me: Please?

Mom: Uh-uh.

Me (kissing her on the cheek): Pretty please?

Mom (smiling): No. Get dressed. Breakfast is ready. I'll drive you.

I have no choice. When my mom says no three times, without any hesitation, it's game over. Believe me, I know.

So I get dressed, groaning loudly the whole time because (a) I want her to feel bad for being so heartless that she's making her bruised and battered son go to school after he landed on his head only the day before and put his ex-girlfriend into the hospital, and (b) every move I make really *does* hurt.

When I get downstairs, I see that my mom isn't completely heartless. She's made my all-time-favorite breakfast—waffles with bananas and maple syrup. My appetite, which I thought was missing in action, suddenly reports for duty. I wolf down the waffles and ask for seconds, which, of course, are warming in the oven.

"I thought I would pick you up after school," my mom says. "We can go over to the hospital together and see how Stassi is."

I want to know how Stassi is. I want desperately to know that she's okay. But...

"I don't know, Mom. What if—?"

"I don't know what happened between you two, Kenzie, and it doesn't matter. All I know is you and Stassi were close. Going over to the hospital is the right thing to do. If things were reversed, Stassi would go to see you. You know she would."

I don't argue with my mom, but I know she's wrong. Before we broke up, no question that Stassi would have been at the hospital. She would have insisted on being there 24/7. But now? After what I did? And I don't mean the accident.

I mean before that. But I know my mom won't let me stay away from the hospital any more than she would let me stay home from school. I know that, no matter what, no matter how I try to dodge it or run away from it, it's going to happen. I am going to have to go.

So I say okay, sure.

Mom drives me to school. She has some kind of built-in anti-tardy device, so, like always, we get there well before the bell rings. She waves to me as she pulls away from the curb, abandoning me to the stares of everyone on the sidewalk. They're all staring at me like I'm a pathetic loser. Even T.J., my best friend, shakes his head as he lopes over to me.

"If it isn't Wrong-Way Korrigan," he says, slapping me on the back. "Oh, sorry, man," he says when I wince. "I heard you went right over the handlebars and landed on Stassi. Great landing! Wish I'd seen the whole thing."

"Stassi's in the hospital," I tell him.

"Yeah, well, from what you've been saying about her, it couldn't have happened to a bigger bi—"

He breaks off when Mandi Fuller butts between him and me.

"Kenzie!" She throws her arms around me, which I hate. She's always doing stuff like that. "I heard what happened. I can't believe she walked into you like that." She pulls back a little and looks me over. "Are you okay? You didn't break anything, did you?"

Just Stassi, I think.

"Stassi's still in the hospital," I say.

"I know," she says.

I give T.J. a pleading look over the top of Mandi's head.

"Hey, Mandi," T.J. says right away. "Me and Kenz got stuff to talk over. Think you could be a pet and buzz off?"

Mandi scowls at him.

"I'm sure Kenzie would appreciate someone *understanding* to talk to," she says.

"Actually, Teej is right," I say. "We have some stuff we have to do. Okay?"

I should just come right out and tell her to get lost, but I can't, not like T.J. can. Sometimes I think there's just too much of my mother in me. Stassi used to say it was one of my best qualities. I feel sick when I think about her. I wonder what's happening with her this very minute. I wonder if she's awake. I wonder if she remembers what happened, if she knows it was me. If she does, I wonder if she hates me more than ever.

Mandi kisses me on the cheek. T.J. snorts. Mandi walks away. I wipe the kiss off my face. T.J. nudges me and gestures with his head. Mandi has seen me wipe away her kiss. Well, so what? Who asked her to kiss me in the first place?

Things go okay for a while.

Kids stare at me, but why not? Everyone has heard about my spectacular run-in with Stassi. Most of the staring is just curiosity—I have scrapes and bruises on my hands and arms, and a big scrape on one cheek. I get a few acid looks, but they're from girls mostly, friends of Lacie Bellows, and those looks don't have much to do with my crash. Lacie is Stassi's best friend, and she just flat-out hates me ever since Stassi and I broke up.

I get questions about what happened—who wouldn't, in my place? Things like, What did the cops say? Is it true I might get charged with careless driving? Do I know how Stassi is? It's the kind of stuff I'd ask if it had been someone else who had flown over their bike handlebars in front of school.

Then, at lunchtime, T.J. and I are heading down to the cafeteria when we run into a bunch of girls. One of them turns to look at me, and I see that she's crying. One by one the others turn, and I see that they're all either crying or have been crying—all except one, a girl named Karyn.

"Nice going," she says, glowering at me like if it was legal, she'd strangle me.

I get a sick feeling in my stomach.

"What now?" T.J. asks. "Did what's-his-name get voted off that stupid talent show?"

Karyn gives him the same look she just gave me and then flicks her gaze back to me.

"Stassi's mom just called Lacie," she says, spitting the words at me.

I glance at Lacie. Tears are streaming down her cheeks. The girls on either side of her have their arms around her waist.

"And?" I say. I can't stand that she's telling me something but not telling me everything. I'm not an idiot. I know something bad has happened.

"And she said Stassi might have suffered permanent brain damage," Karyn says. "I hope you're happy!"

What? Happy? Why would that make me happy? What does she think I am?

"What kind of brain damage?" I ask. "What do you mean, permanent?"

"What do you think, Einstein?" Karyn says. "What happened? You saw her with Logan again, and you decided if you couldn't have her, no one else could?"

"What are you talking about?"

"Right," Karyn says, all snide and sarcastic. "Like you have no idea!"

"I don't," I say. "I would never hurt Stassi. I love her."

Karyn snorts. She looks at the rest of the girls, who are all staring at me like I just got caught with my pants down around my ankles.

"She dumped you," Karyn says. "She dumped you for Logan McCann."

I love Stassi, and I hate Logan. It never bothered me that every girl in school turns to look at him when he walks down the hall. What do I care how hot he supposedly is? I don't. At least, I didn't until Stassi landed the female lead in the school play opposite Logan. Because I was one of the set guys, I had to watch them rehearse and see the way they looked at each other. At first I thought they were just acting. But after a while I thought, no one at this school is that good an actor—not Logan, not Stassi. So when Stassi started saying she had to meet Logan for extra rehearsals, that he was helping her and she wanted to do the best job ever, that she didn't want to stand up there on opening night and embarrass herself, I didn't believe her.

"She didn't dump me," I say. And it's true—sort of. I told her that she had to make up her mind. I told her I didn't mind the scheduled rehearsals when the drama teacher was there, but no more extra practices with Logan. She had to stop those or we were through. I still remember the look on her face. I remember how her voice shook when she said, "*You* don't *mind*?" I remember the passion in her eyes when she told me how important this was to her. I also remember that she didn't try to stop me when I told her, "Fine, we're through," and walked away. I remember that best of all.

I stare at Karyn and the rest of the girls, but I don't know what else to say. I spin around because all I want to do is get out of there—and I slam right into Mandi. I push past her and start to run. I'm halfway down the hall when a hand falls on my arm. I start to jerk away from it. Then I see it's T.J. He leads me outside and finds a corner where we can be alone.

"It wasn't your fault," he says. "It was an accident."

I look at the ground and see Stassi's head with a pool of blood under it.

"Yeah," I say. "An accident."

Chapter Five

I don't know how I get through the rest of the day. My feet take me to my classes, which I enter without looking at anyone. I sit down and stare at my desk all afternoon. No one says a word to me, but I swear I can feel all those eyes drilling into me, and I imagine they are all thinking what Karyn is thinking—that it's all my fault that Stassi is in the hospital. And they're right. It *is* all my fault.

None of my teachers call on me, not even Mr. M, who always picks on me, even though he knows the chances I will have the right answer are, at best, about five percent. I don't bother to go to my locker after the last class. Homework is the last thing on my mind.

My mom is waiting for me outside the school. I can tell by her face that she's heard the news, and she can tell the same thing from mine. But she doesn't say anything until I'm in the front seat beside her. Then she says, "Oh, Kenzie, I'm so sorry."

She reaches over and wraps me in her arms. I start to cry.

"I want to see her," I say.

"I don't know if she's allowed to have visitors," my mom says. "But let's go and see, okay?"

We drive to the hospital, where it takes forever for Mom to find a place in the crowded parking lot and then to guide the car into it. She hates parking lots. She complains the spaces are always too small. She's afraid to scrape the car, which she did once, last year. Dad has never stopped talking about it. Now she's nervous every time she has to park. I don't blame her.

We go through the main entrance, and Mom asks a woman at the information desk where we can find Nastasia Mikalczyk. We are told the room number. Mom leads me through a maze of hallways to some elevators, and we ride up. She finds the right wing and asks again about Stassi. A nurse points the way.

Stassi is in one of those rooms that is glassed in instead of having real walls. She is hooked up to wires and monitors. There is a breathing tube taped to her mouth. Her eyes are closed, but even with all that, she is still beautiful.

Her mother is sitting beside her bed, holding her hand. She looks up when Mom and I approach, as if she feels us coming. She stands, a stunned look on her face. Her eyes go from me to my mom. Then she looks over my shoulder and her eyes widen, like she is afraid of something.

I turn.

Mr. Mikalczyk is coming out of an elevator holding two cups of coffee. He stops when he sees my mom and me. His eyes zero in on me.

"What are you doing here?" he demands in accented English. His voice is loud enough that a nurse at the far end of the hall turns to look at him.

"I...I..." The words won't come out.

"Kenzie wanted to see how Stassi is doing," my mom says. She sounds calm enough to someone who doesn't know her that well, but I notice that her voice is higher than usual. That means she's nervous.

"Get out of here," Mr. Mikalczyk says. He is gripping the cardboard coffee containers so hard that the lid pops off one of them and coffee splashes on the floor.

Mrs. Mikalczyk appears beside him. She takes the coffee from him and sets them on a chair. She wipes his coffee-covered hand with a tissue.

"Tadeusz, please," she says.

But Mr. Mikalczyk still has me in his sights.

"My girl is a vegetable because of you," he says. "Why don't you just kill her and get it over with?"

"Tadeusz!" Tears spring to Mrs. Mikalczyk's eyes. She glances over her shoulder at Stassi lying all hooked up to machines in that bed. "Tadeusz, how can you say that?"

"Well, it's true, isn't it?" Mr. Mikalczyk shouts at her. The nurse at the far end of the hall is coming toward us now. "That's what the doctor said, didn't he?"

"He said there was some damage." Mrs. Mikalczyk is whispering as if she's afraid that Stassi will overhear. "He said we won't know exactly what's going on for a few more days."

But Mr. Mikalczyk isn't listening to her.

"Get out of here," he says to me.

"Mr. Mikalczyk, please," my mom says. "Kenzie just wants—"

"I don't care what Kenzie wants," Mr. Mikalczyk shouts at her, startling her so that she jumps back a little. "*I* want him out of here. Now!" To make his point, he shoves me.

"Keep your voices down, please," the nurse says. She's right beside us now, and she sounds annoyed that she has to tell a bunch of grown-ups—and me—

to keep a lid on it. "Any more shoving or yelling and I'll have to call security."

"Then make him go," Mr. Mikalczyk tells her. "He's the one who put my Stassi in that bed. Get him out of here."

The nurse looks at me. There's no expression in her eyes. My mom takes one of my hands. She tugs on it, and I stumble after her toward the elevators. Mr. Mikalczyk watches us every step of the way. He looks like he wants to kill me. Finally we're inside, and the elevator doors slide shut. Neither my mom nor I say a word the whole way home.

I'm lying on my bed, staring at the ceiling and wishing that everything was back the way it used to be before the stupid play, when someone taps on my bedroom door. It's my mom.

"Mandi is here to see you," she says.

"Tell her I'm sleeping."

"She's worried about you, Kenzie."

I go downstairs and step out onto the porch.

"What do you want?" I say. I don't even try to be friendly, because all I want is to be alone.

"I—" Her face turns red. "I just wanted to see how you are."

"How do you think I am?" I say. "I just put my girlfriend into the hospital."

"Your *ex*-girlfriend," Mandi says in a soft voice.

"I never should have let her go."

"She was cheating on you, Kenzie. You saw it yourself."

"She says she was just rehearsing," I say.

I believe that now. I don't know what made me doubt it. That's not right. I do know. I was jealous. Every girl in the whole school dreams about going with Logan—and Stassi ends up opposite him in a play where he gets to kiss her in front of everyone. Also, from what I could see, he enjoyed rehearsing those scenes way too much. So when Stassi told me they were rehearsing outside of regular rehearsal hours, all I could think about was him wrapping his arms around her and kissing her. It made me crazy. I wanted him to stop. I wanted her to refuse to let him touch her.

What an idiot I was. It's a play. That's all. She kept saying she loved me. Why didn't I believe her? Why did I let myself get so crazy and jealous? Maybe if I'd believed her, I would have been at that rehearsal instead of blowing it off. Maybe I would have been with her. That way I wouldn't have crashed into her.

"She wasn't *just* rehearsing," Mandi says. "I saw them together, Kenzie. I heard her. She was going to dump you once and for all. I'm glad you did it first."

"What? What do you mean? What did you hear?"

"I heard her talking on the phone. She said she was going to dump you."

"Who was she talking to?"

"I don't know. But I heard her loud and clear."

"When? When did you hear that?"

"Last week. Just before you broke up with her."

"No way. You're wrong."

"I know what I heard, Kenzie. You did the right thing. She never appreciated you anyway."

My dad's car turns into the driveway and stops so suddenly that it rocks back and forth a little before he gets out. He slams the door and thumps up the porch steps. He doesn't say anything, but he glowers at me as he goes by. The front door bangs shut behind him.

"You've got to be kidding," he says to my mom. His voice is loud.

I can tell he's angry. "Why didn't you call me?"

"What would you have done?" my mom says. She's perfectly calm.

"Called Howard, for one thing."

"What for?"

"What for?" My dad shouts the words at her. "What for? What do you think I'd be doing if some kid went the wrong way on a one-way street, struck Kenzie and turned him into a vegetable?"

"No matter what anyone says, I'm with you, Kenzie," Mandi says. She bites her lower lip and looks at me like she's trying to figure something out. Finally she says, "I would never cheat on you, Kenzie."

"What?" What is she talking about? How can Mandi cheat on me? We're not even together.

"I really like you, Kenzie," she says slowly. "I—I always have. No matter what. And...well, wasn't I there for you when Stassi cheated on you and lied to you? Didn't you say I was a good friend then? And didn't you..." She blushed. "You kissed me, remember, Kenz?

Yeah, I said it. And I did it. I kissed her. It's embarrassing to remember. I did it because I was so mad at Stassi. We had that huge fight, I told her she had to choose, and she walked away. That afternoon I saw her crying, and she let Logan hold her to comfort her. So when she turned her head, I grabbed Mandi and kissed her. I really kissed her, if you know what I mean. But I don't want to think about that, so instead I say, "Lied to me? Stassi never lied to me."

"She said she wasn't interested in Logan, didn't she?" Mandi says.

"Look, Mandi—"

"But I would never lie to you, Kenzie." She presses herself against me and goes up on her tiptoes so that she can kiss me—on the mouth. I'm so surprised that I push her away.

"Mandi, I'm not...I mean, I don't want..."

"Don't want what?" she asks.

Mandi and I look at each other.

"I love Stassi."

"You just feel bad about what happened," she says. "You don't love her. Not after what she did." She tries to kiss me again. Again, I shove her away.

"Stop it!" I say. "Leave me alone!"

"But—"

"I mean it, Mandi. Leave me alone. I made a mistake. I'm sorry. I don't love you or anything like that. I...It's all my fault. I never should have let Stassi go."

Her face turns red. Her lower lip quivers. Her eyes get all watery. Just my luck, she's going to cry.

"I have to go," I say quickly. I don't wait for her to answer. I go inside, where my mom and dad are still arguing.

"They don't know that for sure," my mom is saying to my dad. "She might be okay."

"For Pete's sake, Susie. If there was a chance she was going to be okay, her folks would have said so. If I were them, if this happened to me, I'd be on the phone to a lawyer. I'd be getting the best advice I could on how I could sue the little hooligan who did this to my son. I'd be figuring out how I could take his parents for everything they were worth. It's negligence, Susie. Carelessness. Maybe all the criminal court can do is slap him with a fine. But the civil court? I'd sue for sure. And I bet that's just what the Mikalchuks are going to do." A moment later, I hear my dad yell into the phone: "Howard, I think we may have a problem."

Chapter Six

My mom calls me for supper. I yell back that I'm not hungry. She doesn't call me again. I hear knives and forks chinking against plates. I smell chicken. My mouth waters. My stomach rumbles. But what kind of guy sits down and eats a hearty supper after he's just given someone permanent brain damage? I lie facedown on my bed and hold my pillow tightly around my head, trying to block everything out. If only I could stop my brain from playing those pictures over and over again—Stassi lying on the sidewalk, the paramedics bending over her, Stassi being loaded into the ambulance.

The doorbell rings. The front door opens, and my dad says, "Howard, thanks for coming."

They must go into the living room, because after that all I hear is the rumble of two deep male voices. It's at least an hour later before I hear the front door open and close again, followed by footsteps on the stairs and a knock at my bedroom door.

"Kenzie? Are you awake?"

It's my dad. I tell him to come in.

"Rough day, huh?" he says as he sinks down onto the edge of my bed.

Is he kidding? *Rough* day? How about the worst day of my entire life?

"You holding up okay?" he asks.

This is why he came into my room? To ask me one stupid question after another?

"Howard Grossman was here," he says.

Here we go.

"He says he doesn't think we have anything to worry about."

I sit up. I want to scream. I want to hit something. But I hold it in.

"He says he doesn't even think the Mikalchuks will try to sue. And if they do, he doesn't think they'll get very far. You're just a kid. It was a stupid accident. And he checked out that sign at the corner. It's almost completely obstructed. He checked out police reports too. At least three motorists have been ticketed for making a wrong turn at the same corner—and they all said they didn't see the sign. He says if anyone is responsible for what happened, it's the city for not making sure that the sign was clearly visible. So, worst case, you'll get a fine."

He's smiling by the time he gets to the end of his little speech, which makes me want to scream even more. Doesn't he get it?

"She's got a head injury, Dad," I say. I try to keep calm, but my voice is high like a girl's, and it's shaky. "Her dad says she's never going to be the same. Stassi is never going to be Stassi again. And you think the worst case is that I'll get a stupid fine?"

My dad pulls back a little. He's startled and, I think, afraid of what I might do.

"All I meant was—"

"I know what you meant, Dad. Howard thinks you're not going to get sued. I'm happy for you, Dad. Really, I am." The truth is, I couldn't care less. "But I love Stassi, and because of me, her life is ruined. You get that, right, Dad?"

My mom appears in my room. I know she's heard every word.

"Oh, Kenzie," she says. She doesn't say anything else, and I love her for that. I know that she, at least, understands what I'm talking about. Like I said, my mom is a people person. A lot of times, that makes her way smarter than my dad.

My dad blinks. He doesn't know what to do. He never knows what to do when people get all emotional. He stands up. He looks at me. He opens his mouth, but I guess he can't figure out what to say, because he shuts it again. He leaves the room. My mom wraps her arms around me again and hugs me. It doesn't make the hurt go away. It doesn't make me less scared. But I'm grateful all the same.

T.J. comes to pick me up the next morning, and we walk to school together. He tries to get a conversation going, first about baseball, then about TV. When that fizzles out, he gives up. We walk in silence. But I'm glad he's with me.

People stare at me, of course.

A half hour before lunch, one of my teachers gets a call on the classroom phone and then tells me I'm supposed to go down to the office. He looks puzzled, so that tells me he doesn't know who wants me or why. T.J. jabs me in the ribs when I pass his desk. I wince, for real. I'm thinking that probably I'm going to get in trouble for ditching drama class without a written excuse. Ms. Rego is probably mad at me for what happened to Stassi.

It turns out the cops are in the office. Not uniformed cops, but the two detectives who showed up at the hospital. Mr. Pawls, the principal, is with them. He tells me the cops want to talk to me. He also tells me that I should call my parents before I say anything to them.

"I'm supposed to call my lawyer," I say.

One of the detectives raises an eyebrow. "You have a lawyer, Kenzie?" he says.

"My dad said I should have one. He says I'm supposed to call him if you want to talk to me again."

"Why does your dad think you need a lawyer?" the other detective says.

Before I can say anything, Mr. Pawls steps in. "He's a juvenile," he says. "You have to inform him of his rights."

The first cop sighs. He says that they want to talk to me about Stassi. He says that I don't have to talk to them if I don't want to. He says if I do talk to them, I have the right to have my parents or some other adults, like a lawyer, present. Then he asks me, do I want to call someone?

"I'm supposed to call Mr. Grossman," I say.

Mr. Pawls leads me behind the counter. I lift the receiver of a phone on one of the office assistants' desks. Then I realize that I forgot to put Mr. Grossman's card in my pocket. I look helplessly at Mr. Pawls. He says he'll get the number for me, then asks one of the assistants to do it.

"What's the problem, anyway?" I say to the detectives while I wait. "My lawyer says I'll just get a fine."

The two detectives glance at each other. Then one of them looks me in the eye and says, "We have a reports that you ran into Stassi Mikalczyk on purpose."

"What?" They have to be kidding. "Why would I do that?"

"That's what we want to know, Kenzie," the detective says. "You and Stassi used to go out, right? She was your girlfriend, and then you broke up. Right?"

"You don't have to answer that, Kenzie. You don't have to say anything to them," Mr. Pawls says.

"He's right," the detective says. "You don't have to talk to us. And you have the right to have an adult present—your lawyer, your parents, even Mr. Pawls—if you do decide to talk to us. You understand that, right, Kenzie?"

I nod. Yeah, I understand. But that's not the point.

"I would never hurt Stassi," I say.

"Kenzie," Mr. Pawls says, like he's warning me to keep my mouth shut. But he doesn't get it. I didn't do it on purpose.

"What report?" I ask. "Who says I ran into Stassi on purpose?"

The detective doesn't answer my question. Instead he says, "I understand that Stassi was doing a co-op program this year. Is that right, Kenzie?"

"She was—" Mr. Pawls begins. But he wasn't the one they asked. I was.

"She likes little kids, and she was thinking maybe she'd like to teach kindergarten," I say. "So she was working one afternoon a week at the daycare center across the street so she could see what it was like to spend a lot of time with a bunch of rug rats."

"Was she enjoying it?" the cop asks.

"Yeah. She was always talking about the kids and how smart they were, even when they were barely able to talk." I smile when I think about it. "I used to walk her over there sometimes and stay for a few minutes so she could show me what she was doing."

"When did she work there?" the cop asks.

"Every Wednesday afternoon."

"From when to when?"

"Kenzie, I really think you should wait for Mr. Grossman," Mr. Pawls says.

The two detectives ignore him. They're both looking at me, waiting for an answer.

"She started at one o'clock and she stayed until five," I say. "At least, that's what she was supposed to do. But Stassi always went in early so she could tidy up while the kids were napping and so she could prepare what she was going to do with them when they woke up."

"What time did she usually go in?"

"Twelve thirty, right after she finished her lunch."

"She *usually* went in around twelve thirty?" the cop says, like he's trying to wrap his head around what I just told him.

"She *always* went at *exactly* twelve thirty," I say. "You don't know Stassi. She's like my mom. She has this thing about being on time. It drives me crazy." I stop. "I mean, it used to drive me crazy." I'm thinking that it's never going to drive me crazy again because Stassi won't be Stassi anymore, not if what her dad said turns out to be true. My voice is quieter when I say, "She always headed over there at exactly twelve thirty."

"Headed over? You mean, she crossed the street from the school here to the daycare center on the other side of the street?" the cop says.

"Yeah."

"Just like she was doing on Wednesday, when you ran into her," the cop says, only now it isn't a question.

"Yeah," I say. I start to see what they're up to. "Yeah, just like always. I already told you that, didn't I? But I didn't run into her on purpose. Why would I do that?"

"What can you tell us about Logan McCann?" the cop asks.

Before I can answer, someone knocks on Mr. Pawls's door. It's his assistant.

"There's a Mr. Grossman here," she says.

Mr. Grossman steps into the room, looks at the cops and tells me not to say another word.

Chapter Seven

"You've got to be kidding," my dad says. We're sitting in the dining room—me and my dad, who came home from the office for this, and Mr. Grossman. "Assault?"

"Aggravated assault," Mr. Grossman says.

"Based on what?"

"Based on eyewitness testimony that Kenzie swerved *toward* Stassi, and based on the fact that Kenzie and Stassi recently underwent an acrimonious breakup." Mr. Grossman looks at me. "That means that it was a bad breakup," he explains.

I know what acrimonious means, but I don't tell him that.

"What eyewitness?" I ask instead. "Whoever it is, they're lying."

"I don't know yet," Mr. Grossman says. "I don't even know if it's one eyewitness or more than one. They'll have to tell me. It's at the top of my to-do list to find out and to get a copy of any witness statements. But you're saying you didn't do it, right, Kenzie?"

"Of course he didn't do it," my dad says. Boy, does he look mad.

Mr. Grossman doesn't look at him. "Kenzie, I need to know," he says.

"I didn't do it," I say. "I mean, I hit her. But it was an accident. I didn't see her."

"Okay," Mr. Grossman says. It's as if he believes me, just because I say so. "Okay, let's go over everything again. I want to hear about the breakup. I want to hear about that day. I want to hear everything."

So I go over it again. I tell him all about what happened between Stassi and me. I tell him how I blew off drama that day because I didn't want to see her.

"Why not? Because you were mad at her?"

I nod, and I can see right away that he doesn't like my answer. If I was mad at her, then that might help to prove that I ran into her on purpose.

"And because I didn't want to see her with Logan again," I say.

"Okay. So you blew off drama. And you were hurrying back to school to get to your next class, right?"

"Not exactly," I say.

"What do you mean, *not exactly*?"

"My next class didn't start until one o'clock. I was going back because—" I hesitated.

"Because why, Kenzie?" Mr. Grossman asks.

"Because I wanted to try to catch Stassi before she went for her co-op placement."

Mr. Grossman leans back in his chair.

"I understand that you told the police that she always gets to her placement at twelve thirty," he says in a quiet voice.

I nod. "That's not good, right?"

"What are you talking about?" my dad says. "What's not good?"

"So you knew there was a pretty good chance she'd be crossing the street when you arrived?" Mr. Grossman says.

I could deny it, but what's the point? I nod again.

"What are you saying, Howard?" my dad demands. "Are you saying you think he did it on purpose?"

"I'm just gathering the facts," Mr. Grossman says. He leans across the table toward me. "Kenzie, I need you to think back to when you turned that corner. I need you to think about what you saw and who you saw."

I try, but my mind is a blank. All I can think is, what if whoever saw me is right? What if I did run into Stassi on purpose? Not that I meant to, not really. But what if it was one of those subconscious things—you know, I was mad at her and I saw her, maybe just out of the corner of my eye, and I hit her. Then I think, even if I didn't do it on purpose, what difference does it make? I did hit her. I put her in the hospital. She's never going to be the same again. And no matter how you look at it, no matter how far back you go with it, it's all because of me.

I can't sleep that whole night. It's bad enough knowing that Stassi is in the hospital and that I put her there. It's worse knowing that the police think I did it on purpose, that I *wanted* to hurt her.

I think about that day over and over. I remember racing back to school after ditching drama class. I remember turning up onto Brannigan, where my school is. I even remember registering in my brain that it's a one-way street. I didn't exactly tell the whole truth when Mr. Grossman asked me about that the first time. I knew it was a one-way street. Everyone knew it. But I didn't care. After all, I was on a bike, not in a car. If I thought about it at all, I guess I thought, how much damage could a person do with a bike?

Well, now I know.

But who talked to the police? Who said I did it on purpose?

Maybe the guy in the car, the one who had given me the finger when he saw I was going the wrong way. Yeah, maybe that's what happened. Maybe I really *did* swerve, but I did it to avoid that car. And maybe someone—maybe the driver of the car or maybe someone else—saw me swerve, and that's why they said what they did to the police.

But that doesn't make sense. For sure it rules out the driver of the car as the person who'd talked to the cops. His big gripe would have been that I was going the wrong way and that *he* could have hit *me*. If he had, he'd be in my position. He'd be feeling bad—maybe—that he'd hit some kid on a bike. Or maybe he'd be thinking that I totally deserved it for going the wrong way on a one-way street. He wouldn't have said that I steered my bike into Stassi on purpose. He was gone before it happened.

It had to be someone else.

It had to be someone who knew me. Otherwise, why would anyone think that I would do something like that on purpose?

It also had to be someone who knew Stassi. Someone who knew about the two of us and our history together. Someone who thought I had a grudge against her, a reason to want to hurt her.

That meant it had to be someone from my school.

Logan.

I'd seen him on the steps of the school just before it happened.

It had to be Logan.

He was the one who kept making plays for Stassi.

He was the one who wanted her so badly.

But he already had her. That's why I was so mad in the first place. So what did he have to gain by telling the cops that I tried to hurt her on purpose?

Unless…

Stassi must have told him that she wanted to get back together with me. I feel even worse now.

The worst part of the whole night is that I have to wait. I can't call Logan. I don't have a cell number for him, which means I'd either have to look up his home phone number and call, or I'd have to go to his place and ring the bell. Neither option will go over well with his parents at two in the morning. They won't let me see him or talk to him even if I am crazy enough to try.

I have to wait.

I hate waiting.

Chapter Eight

I get up early—too early to knock on Logan's door or phone his house on a Saturday morning. I tell my mom I'm going out. She puts down her coffee cup and sets aside her newspaper.

"Where are you going?"

"Just for a walk. To clear my head."

She nods. She understands. My mom always understands.

"Will you be back for lunch?"

I tell her, "Definitely."

I walk over to Logan's house, which is halfway between my house and school. There's a little park just up the street, so I hang out there until I see people start to come out of their houses to walk their dogs or wash their cars or take their kids to karate practice or whatever. I wait another fifteen minutes, and then I walk back to Logan's house and ring the doorbell.

Logan answers. He looks at me. "What are you doing on my porch?" he asks.

"Can I talk to you for a minute?" I ask. "About Stassi?"

He yells back into the house that the doorbell was for him and steps out onto the porch, closing the door behind him.

"What about her?"

"You heard what happened, right?"

He gives me a weird look.

"Yeah," he says. "I heard."

"Are you the one who told the cops that I did it on purpose?"

"What?" His eyes pop open like I've just said the very last thing he ever expected to hear. I start to doubt myself until I remember that he's played the lead in every school play since fifth grade—and he's done TV commercials. He's an actor and—I hate to admit it—he's pretty good. "What are you talking about?" he says.

"Someone told the cops that I hit Stassi on purpose. Was it you?"

"Why would I do that?"

"Because she said she wanted to get back together with me."

"She did?" Logan says.

"She called me. She said she missed me and she wanted us to get back together." And I, fool that I am, told her sure, under one condition. She had to drop out of the play and never let that creep Logan touch her or kiss her again. I had felt cold all over when I heard nothing but silence on the other end of the phone. I told her she could think it over. I told her she could give me her answer the next day at rehearsal. Then, before she could say anything, I hung up. I was pretty sure I'd get what I wanted. After all, she'd called me, hadn't she? She'd said she missed me, hadn't she? If she missed me that much, she would drop out of the play. I was sure of it.

I turned out to be wrong.

"So?" Logan said. "What does that have to do with me?"

What was the matter with him?

"So," I say slowly, "maybe you got jealous."

"Of *you*?" He snorts as if that's the most ridiculous thing he has ever heard. "Get real. Why would I be jealeous of you?"

"Because Stassi wanted to be with me, not you."

Logan shakes his head. "Don't you get it? I don't care."

"But you were groping her all the time."

"Yeah, and she pushed me away—all the time," Logan says. "She was always saying that she wanted everything to look real on stage, but when I showed her real, she freaked out and told me to stop."

"Stop? Stop what?"

He rolls his eyes. "Kissing her. You know, *really* kissing her. Really doing anything. I don't know how you put up with her."

"So you weren't—I mean, you didn't...?"

"I didn't care what she did," Logan says. "Why should I? So if you turned her into a vegetable because you thought she and I were getting it on, you're even more of an idiot than I thought." And there is that smirk again.

I don't know what gets to me more—his attitude, his calling Stassi a vegetable like he doesn't care at all, or his calling me an idiot. I'm not proud of what I do next, but I do it anyway. I hit him. In the face. With my fist. I bet he's not proud of what he does either. He screams the minute he sees blood running down his chin.

"You broke my nose," he shouts at me. "You broke my nose!"

His parents come running. I want to take off, but his dad grabs me. I wriggle free. I run home. I don't know why I think I'll be safe once I get there, because I'm not. Two cops show up an hour later—and my dad answers the door. They arrest me for assault. I have to go down to the police station. My dad calls Howard Grossman and tells me to keep my mouth shut until he and my dad get there.

"I mean it, Kenzie. Not a word. You got that?"

I say I do.

My dad and Mr. Grossman show up after the cops put me in a room for questioning.

"Did you say anything to them?" Mr. Grossman asks.

I shake my head.

"You sure? Nothing at all?"

"Nothing." I don't see what difference it would have made if I had said something. This time I know I'm in the wrong. I knew it when I was doing it. Whatever happens, I'm going to deserve it—this time.

"You want to tell me what happened?" Mr. Grossman asks.

I look at my dad. He's going to get mad when he hears.

"Does *he* have to be here?" I ask Mr. Grossman. "I mean, you're *my* lawyer, right?"

"That's right," Mr. Grossman says. He turns to my dad. "If he wants to speak to me alone, he has that right, Dave."

My dad stares at me.

"You have something to hide, son?"

"I just want to do this myself," I tell him. "With my lawyer."

"Who I'm paying for," my dad says.

"You want me to pay for him?" I say angrily. "Fine. I will."

"Whoa now," Mr. Grossman says. His voice is soft. "Sometimes a boy needs to speak to someone, uh, objective."

"Yeah," I say. "Objective." As in, someone who won't yell at me and ask me what on earth I was thinking.

"Fine." My dad stands up. He walks out of the small room and slams the door behind him. And he tells *me* all the time to stop acting like a kid!

Mr. Grossman doesn't comment. He takes out his writing pad and his fountain pen.

"Now, Kenzie," he says. "What happened?"

I tell him the whole story. I tell him I know I shouldn't have punched Logan but, really, he asked for it. Well, okay, so he didn't *actually* ask for it. But he should have known better than to say what he said. Plus, I'm pretty sure he's the one who ratted me out to the cops for something I didn't even do.

Mr. Grossman puts down his pen.

"Is that why you went over there? Because you think Logan McCann is the eyewitness who says you swerved into Stassi on purpose?"

"Well, yeah." Then I think about what he just said. "What do you mean, I *think* he's the eyewitness? He is, isn't he?"

Mr. Grossman shakes his head.

"All you've succeeded in doing is making the eyewitness statement more plausible. It's clear you were jealous of Logan. It's clear you were angry when you thought that he and Stassi were, uh, an item. It gives you an even stronger motive. So do us all a favor, will you, Kenzie? Stay put, keep your mouth shut and let me see what I can do about getting you out of this mess."

"Who *is* the eyewitness?"

"Uh-uh," Mr. Grossman says. "Look at what you did when you thought it was Logan."

"I promise I won't do anything. I just want to know."

"I'm not going to discuss it, Kenzie." He stands up. "You stay put. I'm going to talk to those detectives and explain to them what happened. Okay?"

He leaves the room, and my dad comes in.

"Well?" he says, dropping down into a chair opposite me. "Did you tell all your secrets to Howard?"

"I don't have any secrets, Dad." I have a thought. "Dad, you know I'd never hurt Stassi on purpose, right?"

"I'd like to think you wouldn't, son. But after what that girl told the police, it's going to be a hard sell."

Girl? It was a girl? What girl?

"I don't care what she thinks she saw," I say to my dad. "She's wrong." I wait a moment. "Has Mr. Grossman talked to her? Do you know who she is, Dad?"

My dad shakes his head. "He won't tell me anything."

"Then how do you know it was a girl?"

"Ted Czernak told me."

I shake my head.

"He's the accountant at work," my dad says, shaking his head like

I'm slow-witted. "I talk about him all the time, Kenzie. He said he heard it was one of Stassi's friends who talked to the cops."

"Which friend?"

"He doesn't know. But if you ask me, any friend of the girl you broke up with is going to have a definite bias. But I bet you anything the Mikalchuks believe every word."

I don't bother to correct my dad about Stassi's last name. Instead I think, It has to be Lacie. Lacie is the one who told the police I did it on purpose. "Dad—"

The door opens, and Mr. Grossman comes back with the two detectives. They want me to tell them exactly what happened. Mr. Grossman nods, so I tell the story again. They finally agree to let me go with a promise to appear. They also tell me to stay away from Logan McCann. I tell them that will be no problem. I can't wait to get out of there. I can't stop thinking about Lacie.

My dad takes me home. He makes sure I stay there. Mr. Grossman tells me he'll talk to me again early next week after he's had some time to sort things out. I head up to my room, but I feel like I'm going to go crazy if I don't do something.

Chapter Nine

I think hard. Lacie told the police she saw me swerve into Stassi on purpose. Why would she do that, especially when it's not true? I don't even remember seeing her on the street that day. But everything happened so fast. There was probably a lot of stuff I didn't see. A lot of people too.

My mom comes into my room.

"We have to go out, Kenzie," she says. "Your dad has those tickets—" Tickets to see Dylan. You'd never know it to look at him, but my dad is a huge Bob Dylan fan. He sees him every time he comes through town. And these tickets are the best—my mom wangled them out of a guy she used to date who's now the program manager at an oldies radio station. They're second-row seats, if you can believe it.

"I'll be fine," I say.

"And you'll stay put?"

"I'll stay put." I feel lousy lying to my mom, but if I don't, she won't leave. And if she doesn't leave, I won't be able to either.

"You promise? Because your dad has his heart set on this, and once the show starts—"

"Nothing will happen, Mom. I promise." In fact, if all goes well,

I'll be back in my room in my pajamas before the show is even half over.

I wait until they leave. Then I wait some more, until I'm sure the warm-up act has left the stage and old Bob is up there doing his thing.

I don't sneak out. There's no need. I walk out like any normal person, locking the door behind me. I go directly to Lacie's house.

She isn't home. Her dad, who doesn't have a clue who I am, tells me she's at a friend's house.

"Karyn's place?" I ask.

"You must know her pretty well," her dad says.

I thank him and make the longer trek to Karyn's place. The two of them are sitting on Karyn's porch. Karyn spots me first and nudges Lacie. They both stand up, Karyn in front and Lacie behind her.

"What do you want?" Karyn says.

"I want to talk to Lacie."

"Yeah, well, Lacie doesn't want to talk to you."

I look around Karyn to Lacie. "You told the cops I hit Stassi on purpose. Why did you do that?"

"Why do you think she did it?" Karyn says, like I'm some kind of idiot. "Because it's true."

"No, it isn't." I look at Lacie again. "I would never hurt Stassi."

"Right," Karyn says snidely. "So she's in the hospital because...?"

"It was an accident. I would never hurt her on purpose." I have to move to the side a little to get a clear view of Lacie. "I don't know what you saw, but it didn't happen that way."

"You're talking to the wrong person, Kenzie," Lacie says in a quiet voice.

"Wrong person? What do you mean?"

Lacie looks at Karyn, who shrugs.

"Go ahead, tell him," Karyn says. "He's going to find out anyway."

Lacie steps out from behind her.

"I didn't see anything," she says.

"But you—" I begin.

"Someone told me what *they* saw. But they were afraid to go to the police. So I told the cops, and they went to talk to her."

Her? Another girl.

"She told them what she saw. She's the one who said she saw you hit Stassi on purpose."

"She who?" I ask.

"Mandi."

Sherlock Holme's idiot brother could predict where I'd go next. I go straight to Mandi's house. Her mom answers the door. She frowns when she sees me.

"Is Mandi here?"

"I don't think she wants to talk to you," Mrs. Fuller says.

"Who is it?" Mandi calls. Before her mom can answer, Mandi bounds down the stairs. She looks uncomfortable when she sees me.

"I need to talk to you," I say.

"I'm busy," she says.

"Okay. I'll say it right here and now. I want—"

"Okay," she says, cutting me off. She turns to her mom. "I won't be long."

She comes out onto the porch and shuts the door behind her, but her mother watches through the window. Mandi nudges me off the porch and down the walk.

"What do you want?"

"Why did you tell the cop I hit Stassi on purpose?"

"Because that's what I saw."

"It's not true."

"I didn't want to tell them, Kenzie. I didn't want to get you in trouble. But you hurt her bad. She's never going to be the same. I couldn't keep quiet about that, could I?"

"But it's not true," I say again.

She steps toward me.

"If you want me to, I can tell them I made a mistake," she says. "I can say I thought it over and that it was an accident. I can say that if you want me to, Kenzie."

It takes me a moment to realize what she means. Then I think, This can't be happening to me.

"I want you to tell the truth, Mandi," I say. "I don't want you to make up stuff. I want you to tell them exactly what you saw." Then I add, "Or what you didn't see."

"I really like you, Kenzie," she says. "I don't want you to get in trouble because of anything I say. I'd really like us to be friends, you know?"

"I'd like us to be friends too, Mandi. But that's all. Just friends. I—I like you too. But not the same way I like Stassi."

She steps away from me.

"I know what I saw," she says. "I really think I should tell them the truth. I'm sorry, Kenzie. If we were close, I guess things would be different. But since we're not..."

She turns and starts back up the walk.

I grab her by the arm.

Her mother opens the door.

I let Mandi go. I am not going to make the same mistake with her that I made with Logan.

Chapter Ten

I'm on the phone with T.J.

"I wish I'd been there," he says. "I wish I'd seen the whole thing. Look, Kenz, if she can lie, I guess I can too."

"I don't want anyone to lie," I say. "I want everyone to tell the truth. I especially want Mandi to tell the truth."

T.J. is telling me he always thought she was a little off when my dad appears in my room. I guess he doesn't notice I'm talking to T.J., because he says, "Do I look like I was born yesterday?"

I look at his receding hairline, his paunch and the crow's-feet at the corners of his eyes.

"Not to me, you don't," I say.

He takes the phone from my hand, proving I was wrong about him not noticing. He holds it up, his face a question mark.

"T.J.," I tell him.

My dad holds the receiver to his ear.

"Goodbye, T.J.," he says.

He closes my phone and tosses it on the desk.

"Irshad saw you leave the house," he says.

Irshad Kirpal is our across-the-street neighbor.

"You *spied* on me?" I say, all indignant.

"You lied to me," my dad says. "And to your mother. You said you wouldn't go out."

"Dad, I—"

But it's too late. He's in full rant, telling me how I'm in enough trouble already and I don't need any more, and if I think the cops are bad, wait until I get a load of what he can be like. Telling me if I went out there and got into another fight with some other kid, he's going to come down on me like a ton of bricks. Telling me, oh, by the way, you're grounded until further notice—except for school. Telling me he hopes I'm clear on that, because if I'm not, I'm going to be sorrier than I've ever been in my life.

He slams the door on the way out.

My mother comes in ten minutes later to kiss me goodnight. She doesn't say anything, but I can tell she's disappointed. After all, she's the one I lied to.

But I don't spend a lot of time thinking about that. Mostly I think about Mandi.

Grounded turns out to mean I can't use the phone. I can't even answer it when T.J. calls the next day. My dad confiscates it and tells me he'll give it back to me when he's good and ready.

Grounded also means chores. My dad sends me to clean out the garage. When I've finished that—he keeps it pretty clean—he sends me downstairs to clean out the basement. That takes all of twenty minutes. My parents are neat freaks. My dad is worse than my mom on that score. Annoyed, my dad tells me to ask my mother for something to do. She gets me to help her make a cake for my dad and frost it with chocolate icing. She puts the radio on while we work, and we have a great time. My dad harrumphs at her, but he doesn't yell. He loves chocolate frosting.

We have the cake for dessert that night. It's so good that my dad and I each have two pieces, with ice cream. When it's time for bed, he thanks me for the cake.

I lie in bed all that night thinking about Mandi again. I don't know what she thinks she saw, but I know she's wrong. I would never do what she said I did. I think about why it is, when things are already bad, they get worse instead of better. I think about Stassi and why I was stupid enough to be jealous of her and Logan together when it turns out that Logan doesn't even care. I think about how I hurt her—really and truly hurt her—and how, when it comes right down to it, it doesn't matter whether I did it on purpose or not. It won't change things for her. It will only change things for me. I think maybe I deserve something bad to happen to me after what has happened to her.

I think about what a jerk I've been. She'd called me and said she wanted us to get back together. She'd missed me. And instead of taking that for what it was, I gave her an ultimatum. Him or me. But really, she wasn't choosing between him and me. She was choosing between having a boyfriend who should have been proud of her for landing the female lead in a play and a boyfriend who was so jealous he couldn't understand that she could do what she wanted and still be the best girlfriend a guy ever had. She was choosing between the me she had fallen in love with and the me that jealousy had turned me into.

I was such an idiot.

I think how much I want to see her. I want to help her too, no matter how badly she's hurt. But her folks won't let me. They were mad enough when they thought it was an accident. But now? Now that they think I did it on purpose, they probably hate me. I'll never be able to get close to her. I'll never be able to tell her how sorry I am.

I wish someone else had seen what happened. I wish it more than anything, mainly so that I can have a chance to see Stassi.

I also think about my parents. I think about how my mom is always on my side. I remember how she took me to the hospital to see Stassi. I think about how disappointed she was when she heard what I did to Logan. I think about my dad and his ranting. I think how much more of that I'm going to have to hear before this is all over. If there's one thing that's hard to listen to, it's my dad in full rant mode.

I sit up straight in bed.

I wonder...

I jump up, turn on my computer and log onto the Internet.

I can't find what I'm looking for.

I feel like throwing my computer across the room, but I don't. There's no way my dad would replace it. I take another look. There haven't been any new posts in days. Is that good?

All of a sudden, I can't wait for it to be morning.

Finally it's seven o'clock. I dress. I eat breakfast. I leave for school. I even get there early, not that it does any good. All I get for my trouble is a lot of nasty stares. I have to wait for my lunch period, and then I have to go looking. I go up and down the street near my school where there are restaurants. I go into them one by one and look at the kids who are eating there. Naturally, he's in the last place I look.

"Hey, Stoner." I wave.

Kegan Stone, aka Stoner, is sitting alone at a table in a burger joint that's practically deserted, which is pretty much how he likes things. When I call his name, he looks surprised and glances over his shoulder to see who this person is who has the same name as him. That's because even though I know him, I know him mainly because of his website. Everyone knows him because of his website. But he doesn't know me. We've never actually spoken.

I walk over to him and introduce myself. He blinks at me.

"I follow your site," I say. "I love your rants."

He posts them several times a week, and they're always entertaining. He rants about school, about teachers, about the useless stuff we learn. He also rants about the city and politicians, about war and the way people are quick to react to natural disasters but are pretty slow when it comes to man-made ones. He stands outside of the school, points his phone at himself and lets fly with whatever's on his mind.

"You haven't posted one in a few days," I say.

"Yeah, I've been in planning mode," he says. He squints at me. "What did you say your name is?"

I tell him again.

He nods, but his face is blank.

"So," I say, "how long have you been in planning mode? Because I swear I saw you doing a rant last week—Wednesday, in fact. But I don't see it up on your site."

He shrugs. "I was repeating myself. That's when I figured it was time for something new."

"So you did record one last Wednesday?" I'd seen him out on the street, standing across the street from the school, the way he always does. Standing with his back to the school, the way he always does, so that the school is always—always—in the background.

"Yeah, I think so," he says. He pulls out his phone, turns it on and stares at it for a few seconds. "Yeah," he says. "I guess I forgot to delete it."

I see his thumb move toward the Delete button.

I grab the phone from his hand.

"Hey!" he says.

"Can I see it?" I ask. What I'm thinking is, That was close.

He relaxes and shrugs again.

"Go crazy," he says.

I watch the video of his last rant.

There he is, with the school directly behind him, while he talks about exams and how they prove nothing. It's no help at all. Then the phone moves and there's a side view of him saying that all the exams show is that some kids are good at memorizing stuff. Behind him, I can see the buildings up the street. Still no help.

Then the phone moves again.

Again there's a new angle while Stoner talks how the brain doesn't work exactly the same way in every single human being.

I see a white delivery van. I don't listen to Stoner's commentary anymore.

I see someone on a bicycle turn onto the street. It's me.

I see a car go by me and remember the driver who gave me the finger.

I see myself looking over my shoulder at the car.

I see…

It goes by so fast. The next thing I know, the screen is blank.

"I have to see that again," I say.

"Kenzie," he says thoughtfully, like he's only just registering my name.

"Yeah."

"The Kenzie that ran into Stassi?"

I nod.

"Stassi's okay," he says. "She was my girlfriend in kindergarten. Did you know that?"

I have to say that I didn't. Stassi never mentioned it. I knew she liked him though. And she never made fun of him the way some people did. She said he was smarter than he looked. She said he wasn't made for regular school but that someday, all the idiots who made fun of him were going to be surprised. She said he wanted to make movies. She said he would be great at it.

"I need to see this again, Stoner."

He takes the phone from me and fiddles with it, and it plays again. This time he watches it with me.

"Whoa," he says softly just before it ends. "Did you see that?"

"I need you to post this," I say. "And I need you to send it to my phone."

"No problem," he says.

Then I remember that I don't have my phone.

"One more thing," I say. "I need to borrow your phone—after school."

Naturally, he isn't sure about that. I tell him what I want to do. I also tell him why.

"Anything for Stassi," he says.

Chapter Eleven

I meet Stoner after school. Maybe I should have gone directly to the police. But I need to clear this up in my own mind first.

I spot her.

“Wait here until I call you,” I tell Stoner.

He nods.

I wave to Mandi.

She looks at me, uncertain.

"I need to talk to you," I tell her. "About what happened."

"I'm not going to change my mind, Kenzie. I told the police what I saw."

"You have to do what you have to do," I say.

"So what do you want?"

"I want to know why you did it."

"Did what?"

"Lied."

"I already told you—" she begins.

"You lied to me. You told me that you heard Stassi say she was going to dump me the day before I actually dumped her." Stassi had come backstage and said she wanted to be in the play, and she didn't see why that had to come between us. Technically, she had broken up with me. But I was the one who made it happen.

"I told you what I heard."

"Maybe it's just what you wanted to hear," I say. "Stassi called me the night before. She wanted us to be together. She didn't want us to break up at all."

Mandi doesn't say a word.

"I think you should tell the cops the truth, Mandi," I say.

Her eyes look hard when she says, "I already did."

I call to Stoner. Mandi frowns when he walks toward us.

"Show her," I say.

"Show me what?"

Stoner opens his phone and turns it on. He holds it out for her to see. She watches with a sour expression on her face at first. Then she starts to look nervous. When it gets to the part where he's captured her shoving Stassi, pushing her right out into the street, she makes a grab for the phone. Stoner's been expecting that. He jerks it away from her and tucks it safely back into his pocket.

"The cops are going to see that video," I tell Mandi. "You can talk to them first and tell the truth. Or you can wait for them to come knocking on your door."

She starts to cry.

"I didn't mean for it to happen," she sobs. "I just—why does she have to get everything? Why is it never me?"

I know I should be mad, but I'm not. I actually feel sorry for her.

"You have to tell them, Mandi." And then, because I'm a little nervous about what she might do, I tell her that I'll go with her.

"Me too," Stoner says.

I look at him.

"I've got the goods," he says, holding up his phone.

On the way to the police station, Mandi says she's sorry. She says it over and over. She says she didn't mean for it to happen. Yes, she was mad at Stassi. She'd lied to Stassi too. She'd said that

I had asked her out and that I wasn't interested in Stassi anymore. But Stassi said she didn't believe her.

"She's as crazy as you are, Kenzie," Mandi says. "Even after everything, she just wanted to be with you. And she knew in her heart that you wanted to be with her. That's what she said to me. She said, 'I know it in my heart.' And that's when I pushed her. I didn't even see you. I pushed her, and the next thing I knew, someone on a bike ran into her. I was sure I was going to get into trouble, but no one saw me."

Stoner pats the pocket where his phone is.

"No one except Stoner's phone," Mandi says. "I'm sorry, Kenzie. I—I was mad at you too. You pushed me away."

I keep my mouth shut the whole time because I'm afraid if I say anything, I'll get her mad all over again. Not that it matters now that we have Stoner's video.

But I'm tired of everyone being mad at me.

Mandi talks to the cops. Stoner shows them his video and, when they ask him to, sends it to one of the cop's phones. Mr. Grossman shows up because I called him and asked him to. My dad is with him. He's angry, probably because he thinks I did something else stupid. He calms down when he finds out what's going on.

"So Kenzie is good then," he says to Mr. Grossman. "He's not in trouble."

"He's still liable to a fine for the illegal turn onto a one-way street," Mr. Grossman says. "And he's still got that assault charge. But if he pays the fine and apologizes to Logan McCann, maybe he can get away with a suspended sentence."

I'm happy to do whatever I have to as long as someone makes sure to tell the Mikalczyks that I didn't hurt Stassi on purpose. Mr. Grossman agrees to handle that.

Chapter Twelve

I'd like to say that I'm so brave that I turn down my mother's offer to go to the hospital with me the next day. But I'm not that brave. I'm glad she's with me. I even let her do the talking. I'm pretty sure she's nervous too, but she walks up to the Mikalczyks all the same.

"I guess you heard by now what happened," I hear her say. "I guess you know that Kenzie didn't hurt Stassi on purpose."

Mrs. Mikalczyk turns to look at me. She comes toward me. Mr. Mikalczyk starts to follow her, but Mrs. Mikalczyk puts her arm on his and says something quietly to him. I don't understand what she says. She isn't speaking English. She comes to where I'm standing.

"Stassi woke up," she says.

I feel myself shake all over. My mouth is dry. I'm afraid to say anything, afraid to ask.

"She doesn't remember what happened," Mrs. Mikalczyk says. "She can't remember a lot of things."

Poor Stassi. I feel awful. I know that I would never have hit her if Mandi hadn't pushed her out into the street. But that doesn't make things better, not even remotely.